A WITCH COZY MYSTERY

SHORT STORY 1

T. LOCKHAVEN
CATHERINE LACROIX

EDITOR
GRACE LOCKHAVEN

TWISTED KEY
publishing
2024

First Printing: 2024

ISBN 978-1-63911-117-6

Twisted Key Publishing, LLC
www.twistedkeypublishing.com

Ordering Information:
Special discounts are available on quantity purchases by corporations, associations, educators, and others. For details, contact the publisher at the above listed address.

U.S. trade bookstores and wholesalers: Please contact Twisted Key Publishing, LLC by email twistedkeypublishing@gmail.com.

Ophelia Windsor stood outside a one-story house on the outskirts of Cicero, hugging her long coat around her waist. She pressed the small button on the doorbell and waited.

The leaves on the trees had shifted to browns, reds, and yellows, littering the dying grass with vivid sparks of color. Early morning sunlight glittered through the branches, casting long shadows over the house. She murmured beneath her breath, summoning a light breeze to rustle the leaves and weave through the branches. Gentle reminders that the wind would heed her call made visits like this easier. As a witch, visiting a stranger's house tended to go either very well or very poorly.

But this wasn't a 'witch' matter. Not really.

Three, two, one…

Ophelia rang the doorbell again. Why wasn't Ms. Lewis answering? They'd *just* spoken on the phone—Max had made record time and brought Ophelia from her office to this address in less than fifteen minutes.

At last, the door swung open, and a disheveled young woman with dark hair and darker eyes brushed a hand through tousled tangles, panting as she propped open the screen.

She wore a robe of multicolored silk adorned with a blue sash and a necklace with a jade sphere dangling at its end.

"Ms. Madeline Lewis, I presume?" Ophelia asked.

"Yes! Goodness, yes. Hello, Ms. Windsor. I'm so sorry. Please, come in," Madeline stood aside, allowing Ophelia to pass.

Ophelia waited. "You assured me on the phone that you knew our phrase." Only members of Cicero's magic circle were familiar with their passphrase, which helped guarantee a safe place to discuss matters between immortals. Madeline had identified herself as a psychic—a rarer power in the world of magic. Ophelia could count on one hand the number of psychics she knew. It seemed suspicious to have two living in Cicero.

"Oh! Right." Madeline stepped forward, looked to her left, then her right, then chanted in a quick whisper, *"Quem dues vlutperdere, dementat prius."*

"Thank you." Ophelia nodded. *Two psychics in Cicero it is, then.* She made a mental note to catch up with Margie soon. "Who did you say you obtained my number from?"

"Renee Swan. She said you're the best private investigator there is."

More like the only private investigator in Cicero. But that sounds like Renee. "Very well. I'll pass her my thanks."

"Of course. Now, I don't think we have much time, please come in." Madeline beckoned Ophelia inside with a flapping hand and vanished into the hallway. "I was trying to pick up before you came over, but I'm glad you got here so quickly. Since, well, time is of the utmost importance right now."

"I couldn't agree more," Ophelia replied as she stepped across the threshold.

Madeline led them down a congested hallway. A white cat weaved between her ankles, loudly announcing its displeasure at the sudden intrusion. "Please pardon Angus. We don't get many visitors."

Ophelia smiled. "My cat would understand." Figaro was very particular about those who spent more than ten minutes in their apartment. Unless it was Renee visiting. Ophelia's best friend had a way of charming every person and animal she encountered.

They arrived in a small living room with multicolored curtains over white blinds. A square television on a white stand stood as the room's center focus, flanked by a recliner and a loveseat turned to face one another.

Madeline gestured for Ophelia to take the burnt orange recliner on the left. "Please, sit."

A thin layer of Angus's white cat fur painted the seat. Ophelia imagined it on her black coat, her lips pulling into a thin line. Figaro's fur matched her coat, but Angus's would stick out like a sore thumb. "I can stand, thank you."

Madeline frowned, taking a seat on the loveseat across from her.

Ophelia cleared her throat. "It's good to meet another cat enthusiast. Figaro's also selective when it comes to his favorite furniture."

That won a small smile. "Aren't they all? But that's not why you're here. We don't have time for small talk."

Yes, you keep saying that. Ophelia extracted a notebook from her breast pocket. "Of course. What did you see, Ms. Lewis?"

"Maddy's just fine, if you please." Madeline clasped her hands in her lap. Angus leapt up onto the sofa and curled up beside her. "I had a vision. The scene was incredibly vivid. There's going to be a murder. I saw a room with two lines of desks stacked with paperwork and pens. Gray walls, dark carpet. Bright lights—"

"Sounds like an office."

"Yes. I think so. It flashed before me like a fevered dream. This young woman was shouting at the top of her lungs—"

"What did she look like?" Ophelia interrupted, scribbling furiously on her notepad. She wanted to capture every detail possible while Madeline's vision was still fresh in her mind.

"Um, brown hair, I think. Or it could have been red. It was hard to tell how tall she was. Maybe a little shorter than you?"

"Thank you. Where were you in the room?"

"It was like I was a fly on one of the desks watching the exchange. It's hard to describe."

"Understood." Ophelia made a quick note. *Out of body.* "Please continue."

"Well, she kept repeating, 'Why? *Why?*' The other person she was shouting at was hidden by the doorframe. Just a shadow over the woman screaming."

"Was there anyone else in the room besides the woman that you could see?"

"I-I don't believe so." Madeline drummed her fingers on her knee. "If there were others behind me, I wouldn't know."

"Right. Continue."

"There was more shouting. She said, 'Have you lost your mind?' And then there was a gunshot. Then another. She dropped to the floor. Footsteps. The ding of an elevator. And—And I—"

An elevator. So, the building's pretty tall. "And?"

Madeline shook her head. "That's it. My vision ended."

"Was there anything on the desks or walls that could have given you a clue to where they were?"

"I saw paperwork around me, but the writing was so blurry. I couldn't make anything out."

This could be anywhere. Ophelia tapped her pen against her notes. "Could this be somewhere outside of Cicero?"

"My visions have a limit, I think. I've never had them beyond the city, as far as I can tell." She closed her eyes and concentrated. "Oh! There was a photo on the desk that I recognized! It was Garfield Park!"

The conservatory? That was near enough. "But no glimpse of the other person at all?"

"No. And I didn't hear them say anything." Madeline opened her eyes and swept a loose strand of hair behind her ear. "Gee, now that I've actually talked about it, it doesn't really seem like there's much to go on, huh?"

Ophelia chewed her lip. No, this wasn't much to go on at all. "How far in advance do your visions usually take place?"

"Well, whenever I have a vision, it almost always happens on the same day." Madeline fretted at her lower lip. "I don't think I've ever had a vision that happened in the past or in the real far future."

"'*Almost* always'?" Ophelia repeated.

"Yes. Besides… Well, I don't know how to explain it, but this one *felt* like it was going to happen real soon."

"And you said you didn't call the police with this information, correct?"

Madeline puffed her cheeks out and exhaled through a small 'o' shaped by her lips. "The last time I did that, the officer threatened to keep me overnight for my mental health." She glanced at the ceiling. "I don't give anonymous tips anymore."

"Right. Thank you, Ms. Le—Maddy," Ophelia quickly corrected herself. She wasn't sure she would ever grow used to using first names in a professional setting. She pocketed her notebook and stood. "Your assistance is incredibly appreciated. I'll see what I can do, and I'll call you if I need anything." Procuring a business card from her breast pocket, she held it forward for Madeline to take. "If you remember anything else, please give me a call."

"I will." Madeline accepted the card and clapped her hands to her chest. "Please help her, Ophelia. Please."

If only I had eyes on every inch of Cicero. "I'm going to do the best I can." With a final nod, Ophelia left the house and marched back to the taxi. She plucked a tuft of white cat hair from her coat as Max jumped out of the cab and circled around to open the door.

"Back to the office, please, Max," she said as she stepped inside.

"Ya know, Ms. Windsor, I'm not on a first-name basis with many people." Max grinned and closed the door. They'd known one another for nearly a decade, but his manners were always perfect.

"Wouldn't you know it? Neither am I." Ophelia chuckled as he hurried back to his seat. She withdrew a pack of cigarettes from her coat, extracted one, slipped the filter between her lips, and cupped her hands around the flame of her lighter. As she took a slow drag, she considered her options.

Calling Lieutenant Jackson at the station wouldn't help. It didn't matter how many officers he dispatched—how could they arrest someone who hadn't committed a crime? Even

Cynthia, the single immortal on the police force, wouldn't be able to identify it in time. Besides, there was a high chance that wards would not be present at the scene; what Madeline had described seemed like a cold-blooded murder between humans. Plenty of folks got into yelling matches with each other when someone flipped their lid.

However, as Ophelia replayed the short conversation that Madeline recounted, the victim's words *did* make their relationship sound more familiar rather than words screamed at a random furious gunman. There was history there. It wasn't two complete strangers, and the day was still young. Ophelia didn't leave her apartment earlier than six a.m. unless it was a very good reason. If Madeline's gut feeling was right, if the murder was going to happen soon, then she still had time to narrow down the potential businesses in the area with tall buildings.

"Need to burn some rubber, Max," Ophelia said, rolling down the window by an inch and flicking the ash from her cigarette.

"Yes, ma'am." Max tipped his hat and stepped on the gas.

When they arrived back at her office building, she paid Max with a generous tip and hurried inside. Tiffany, the building's bleeding-heart secretary, looked up from her desk and leapt to her feet.

"Ms. Windsor! Oh, Ms. Windsor, I'm so glad you're back." Her quick steps approached Ophelia faster than Ophelia could protest. Behind Tiffany, Julia caught Ophelia's eye from her desk, shrugged, and shook her head. Ophelia tended to rely on Julia for information, for leads, and to keep Tiffany at bay. *Not even Julia could stop her this time.*

Ophelia raised her hand. There wasn't time for another missing dog or personal document search. "Tiffany now is not a good time."

"No. Ms. Windsor, you don't understand." Tiffany halted just inches away, dancing on her tiptoes and writhing her fingers. "There's been a murder! Lieutenant Jackson's on the phone. He's been waiting for you to return." Her Southern Drawl lingered on Jackson's name.

"Alright." Ophelia nodded. "Okay," she muttered, then turned toward the elevator. "Can you transfer him to my office?" she asked over her shoulder.

"Of course, ma'am!" Tiffany's heels clicked as she maneuvered back to her desk.

"Thanks, Tiffany," Ophelia called, but Tiffany's voice had dulled to a murmur as she relayed the news to Jackson and offered to transfer him up.

When she stepped onto the elevator, Ophelia exhaled the tension she'd held since standing in Madeline's living room.

So much for staying ahead of this one.

When Ophelia returned to her office, Lieutenant Simon Jackson was waiting on the horn.

"Hello, Jackson," Ophelia answered, leaning against her desk and gazing out the window. She cradled the receiver against her shoulder while tugging the pack of cigarettes from her coat.

"Ms. Windsor. I assume you heard." Simon's baritone drummed against Ophelia's ear.

"That there was a murder? Yes." Ophelia sighed and lit her cigarette. "Though I believe I knew about it before you this time."

"Something you need to tell me, Ms. Windsor?"

"I received a call this morning from a Madeline Lewis…" Ophelia explained Madeline's vision and her house visit. Jackson knew about the circle and called on Ophelia when cases didn't quite 'feel right.' The Deputy Director was happy to sign her checks so long as the cases were closed. "I'd planned on calling you when I returned, but isn't this a little early for you to be calling *me*?" Jackson only got her on the line when his usual detective hit a seemingly impossible roadblock.

Simon sighed. "Detective Frisbe's out of town. But maybe this one's better in your hands anyway."

A willing turnover? From Jackson? "Truly? Are you feeling alright, sir?"

"Ophelia," he warned.

She took another pull from her cigarette and smiled. "I'm sorry, Jackson." She cradled the phone between her left shoulder and ear and reached for her notebook. "What've we got so far?"

"One Diane Kahler. Forty-one years old. Murdered in her office at Barnard Financial this morning. Time of death approximately seven thirty-five a.m. by a gunshot wound. Three bullets to the chest. Short list of suspects, shorter list of evidence."

"That matches up with Ms. Lewis's vision." Ophelia added Diane's name, the location, and the time beside her notes from Madeline. "Let's start with the suspects."

"First Diane's husband, Jerry Kahler. I have an officer out to speak with him at home, but no evidence at present to bring him in. The second suspect is the security guard on duty, Larry Hall, who would have been in the building at the time. Third is Diane's coworker, Sandy Livingston. Besides Larry, Sandy was the only other person inside Barnard Financial this morning."

"Who discovered the body?"

"Sandy Livingston, I believe. The call into the station was female."

"Got it. So Jerry's at home, but what about Larry and Sandy?"

"Larry's still at the office. Sandy may still be there when you arrive, but it's difficult to say. There's not enough probable cause to bring either of them into custody just yet. Since Frisbe's gone, that job falls to you, Ms. Windsor."

"Right. Of course." The station officers could find out the basics, but it was on Ophelia to do the deeper digging. "Do you have Jerry Kahler's address and phone number handy? I'll start there."

"Yes. One moment." The sound of shuffling paperwork filled the space, and then Jackson rattled off the suspect's contact information.

"Great. Anything else I should know?"

"Not at the moment. If we turn up something, I'll give you a call."

"Sounds good." Ophelia stabbed the butt of her cigarette into a nearby ashtray.

"Before you go, I need to know, should we keep an eye on Madeline Lewis?" Jackson asked.

"I don't believe she's involved," Ophelia replied honestly.

There was a long pause, and then, "I know how you feel about this, Ophelia, but let me keep an officer on watch."

Ophelia worked her jaw, glad that Jackson couldn't see it. That unspoken, 'Just in case,' hung heavy in the air. He was just as superstitious about immortals and the circle as he was understanding. To his credit, they hadn't had the cleanest track record lately. "Can it be Officer Brewer?"

"If you don't believe you'll need her at the crime scene, then yes, I can send Cynthia."

That made her feel a little better. "Alright. Thank you. Got a pen?" Ophelia relayed Madeline's address. "And call Julia if you need me while I'm gone."

"Of course. Thank you, and good luck."

Ophelia ended the call and immediately lifted the receiver. The faster she could get interviews, the better. Too much time granted the guilty an unparalleled storytelling ability, solidified behind a wall crafted by self-assurance and dangerous justification. She dialed Jerry's number and lit another cigarette.

"Hello?" a gruff voice that sounded like the man had just woken up answered on the fourth ring.

"Good morning. Am I speaking with Jerry Kahler?"

"Yeah? This is Jerry." Jerry's voice strained.

Ophelia realized it was the dry rasp of someone who'd spent the last hour crying. "I'm Ophelia Windsor, a private investigator working with Cicero police."

Jerry heaved an exasperated sigh. "Everything I know I told the guy still sitting in my living room. Jeez, my wife just died. Do you people have any compassion at all?"

It's going to be like this, then. Ophelia took a deep breath. Everyone processed grief a little differently; even magic did little to take that edge off. She continued with a softer tone. "I'm terribly sorry for your loss, and I'm certain you did, sir. I want to help you. I won't take up much of your time. I just need a few questions answered."

Five beats of silence, then a dour, "Alright."

"Where were you at seven o'clock this morning?"

"Sleeping."

"Sleeping?" Ophelia blinked. "Do you work an evening shift, Mr. Kahler?" Those were becoming more popular lately.

"No." Jerry made a noise between frustration and disgust, then he snapped, "I'm in-between jobs, *Ms. Windsor.*"

A bit of a sore spot? She noted his unemployment and continued. "I understand. So, just to be clear, your wife woke up on her own, prepared for work, and left while you were still asleep?"

"That's about the score of it, yes."

Ophelia sketched a small timeline. "What time does she usually wake up?"

"Five-thirty or so. Sometimes, it varies. Like I said, I was knocked out."

About two hours between waking up and the time of death. "Thank you. Now, would you kindly describe your relationship with Diane?"

Another pause. "What kind of a question is that? You a shrink?"

Ophelia swallowed his reply and continued, "No. However, I would like to inform you that this conversation will go on the record should it come to court."

Jerry cleared his throat. As it usually went when confronted on a recorded line, his tone improved. "Look. Diane and I were great. The perfect husband and wife team. We were gonna

take on the world together, you know? I just…"
He sniffed, and his voice broke. "I can't believe
she's gone."

Maybe the court threat was a little far.
Ophelia softened her tone. "I know, Mr. Kahler.
I understand that this is a difficult time, and I
know it can be hard to feel like you're under the
spotlight. Your cooperation is sincerely
appreciated."

"Of course. I'm sorry." He sucked in a
ragged breath. "This is just a shock, you
know?"

"I can only imagine." Ophelia tapped her
pen against her notepad. "Is there anything else
you think I should know regarding Diane, Mr.
Kahler? Is there anyone you can think of who
would have wished her harm?"

"Hmm. The other night, she was rattled over
a coworker. She didn't really go into it." Jerry
sighed a forlorn chuckle. "I admit, though, I'm
not a very good listener."

Coworker troubles, Ophelia scrawled down.
"Anyone else?"

"Not that comes to mind, no."

"Alright. I think that about covers it."
Ophelia nodded, then realized he couldn't see
it. "Thank you, Mr. Kahler. We'll contact you
with any new findings. Should you remember
anything else at all, please contact the station."

"Thank you, Ms. Windsor. Really, I appreciate it."

"You're welcome. I'll be in touch." Ophelia disconnected the line and then looked at the next names in her notepad.

Larry and Sandy, huh?

Even with a murder, it was likely the security guard was still in the building. If Sandy was still there for questioning, Ophelia could catch her before she left.

She hoped that Max was still nearby. It'd be an expensive taxi day.

Barnard Financial was a one-story building situated between many of downtown Cicero's skyscrapers. A modest architectural effort that welcomed new customers with subtle colors and pristine landscaping. However, there wouldn't be any customers crossing the yellow caution tape today. Two police officers stood by the front door just a few feet from where the car was parked, lights swirling their warning to anyone driving by. A handful of curious onlookers circled the tape, but two of them shrugged and left when they didn't find anything of interest.

Ophelia introduced herself to the officers, recognizing Officer Jones from other cases she'd worked on. After a quick exchange of greetings, Officer Jones stepped aside and held one glass door open for her. But she didn't get very far before a young man in a security uniform confronted her.

"I'm sorry, ma'am. We're closed today," he said kindly, extending one arm over the second set of double doors.

Ophelia spied more caution tape down one of the long hallways behind the doors and police officers investigating the scene.

"Yes, I'm Ophelia Windsor, a private investigator. I'm working with Lieutenant Simon Jackson on this case." She gestured behind her. "Officer Jones cleared me."

The guard's eyebrows raised. "You're very pretty for a detective."

Ophelia kept her expression neutral. "That's kind of you. Are you Larry Hall?"

He glanced from side to side with a shy smile. "Why? Am I in trouble?"

"Not necessarily," Ophelia countered, pulling her notebook free from her coat. "May I ask you a few questions about Diane Kahler?"

"Oh! Of course, ma'am! Larry Hall, at your service!" Larry started, then offered a salute. "Wait, did you say Diane?"

"Yes, sir."

Larry's face and shoulders visibly slumped, eyes screwing out of focus. "I didn't know it was Diane. Geez." He dragged one hand through his thick, dark hair. "Ain't that a bite?"

"My apologies. I thought one of the officers would have spoken with you already."

"No, they were talking to Sandy all mornin'… Gee whiz. That's a shame."

"Sandy Livingston? Is she still here?"

"No, ma'am. You see, erm…" Larry danced from one foot to the other, looked over his shoulder, then scratched his chin.

Ophelia furrowed her brow. "What is it?"

"Well, the other night— you know, I don't know if I should tell you about this. Don't want to shake up the higher-ups." He pointed to the sky as if his information would upset the heavens themselves.

"Everything you tell me is confidential, Mr. Hall. I assure you." *Surely, you will be forgiven.*

Larry nodded. "Okay… The other night, Sandy and Diane had a big fight. Gosh, Sandy. She fights like a tiger. Anyway, Sandy and Diane were having a go of it. Screaming at the top of their lungs until the boss called on me. I had to escort Sandy out to her car, and I'm pretty sure she was fired for it."

"Ms. Livingston was fired, but she was here this morning?" Ophelia nibbled the end of her pen.

"Yes, ma'am." Larry wrung his hands together and searched the ceiling.

"Do you know why?"

"No, ma'am. Like I said, the officers haven't told me much."

Ophelia scribbled notes while Larry spoke. "And where were you this morning?"

"Standing guard at the door. Just like I always do, ma'am." Larry nodded. "I let the officers in, but no one would tell me what was going on." His eyes dropped to the floor. "Poor Diane."

"So, you saw Diane and Sandy enter the building?" *That would make this easy.*

"Oh, apologies, ma'am. My shift starts after the morning team gets here. Before that, I was at The Cat's, grabbing a cup of coffee." Larry bowed his head. "Sandy was here talking to the officers when I arrived. I'm sorry, ma'am."

"Who was on guard before then?"

Larry scratched his head. "I-I'm the first on call, ma'am."

"There isn't a security guard for the morning team?"

He shrugged. "I'm not here to watch the employees, Ms. Windsor. There's no customers to keep an eye on."

So very close. "Alright, Mr. Hall. When did the fight between Sandy and Diane you referenced happen?"

"Hm. Two nights ago. Yeah, because I went to—I went to Benny's to get a hot dog after work." Larry chuckled. "That's become a bit of a Wednesday haunt for me."

"So you escorted Sandy to her car afterward. Did you see Diane leave the building?"

"I did. As far as I know, she made it home just fine." Larry shrugged.

Ophelia brushed an escaped tendril of black hair behind her ear and squared her shoulders. "Can you tell me more about Diane? Her personality?"

"Diane was one sweet lady. Hard worker. She always took the time to say hello, though. Even baked me cookies a few times. I really liked that."

"Do you think Sandy was capable of harming Diane?"

"N-no, ma'am. More bark than bite, that lady. Well, I mean… I think so, anyway. Gee whiz, do you really think she'd do such a thing?"

"That's what I'm here to find out. Anyone else that you can think of that would have wanted to harm Diane?"

"Golly, I don't think so. But I didn't know her that well, to be honest with you, Ms. Windsor."

"Thank you, Mr. Hall." Ophelia looked around the room, searching for the familiar blinking red light. "Do you have security cameras in this facility?"

"No, ma'am. But I hear those are in the works for later this year."

Ophelia nodded. If she had it her way, everywhere would have a camera and hours of video to sift through. "I appreciate your help, Mr. Hall. Do you know where I can find Sandy right now?"

"Probably at home." Larry shrugged.

"May I please get her address?"

Larry's face blanched, and he adjusted his necktie. The thin gleam of sweat pooling on his brow began to drip tendrils down the sides of his face.

Ophelia narrowed her gaze. "Mr. Hall, I can ask one of these fine officers to acquire it for me if it would make you feel better."

"No! No, that's just fine. You've been nothin' but kind to me. Just a moment." Larry hurried around his desk and sifted through a pile of manila envelopes. He procured Sandy's file and read off her address as Ophelia quickly scratched it down.

"Wonderful. Before I go, is there anything else that you can tell me about Diane Kahler?"

Larry glanced at the ceiling and narrowed his eyes in thought. "No… No, I think that's it."

"Thank you, Larry. I'll be in touch." Ophelia passed a business card to him. "If you can think of anything else, please give my office a call. Or let one of the officers here know."

"Of course, Ms. Windsor. Happy to help." Larry nodded vehemently. "Golly. Poor Diane."

Sandy Livingston next, then. Sounds like a real firecracker.

Sandy's house was an attractive two-story building with a fresh coat of paint and a red brick roof. The lawn was perfectly manicured, with colorful blooms sprouting from the garden. A dark-haired young woman wearing a long skirt and button-up blouse greeted Ophelia at the door.

"Good morning. My name is Ophelia Windsor. I'm a private investigator. Are you Sandy Livingston?"

"No. I'm sorry, Ms. Windsor, I'm the housekeeper." She glanced over her shoulder. "My name is Kate. I can show you to the living room."

Ophelia soon found herself in the sparkling living room with a cup of tea and a staring contest with Sandy's toy poodle.

"Sit," Ophelia said.

The poodle obliged with a tiny whine.

Sandy bounced down the stairs and to the couch opposite Ophelia, positively beaming. Blonde curls framed a soft, pale face, and her makeup was pristine. Sandy's demeanor was that of a woman who had just won a sweepstakes rather than having recently been fired from her job.

"So! What can I do for you, Ms. Windsor?" Sandy asked.

"I have a few questions about the murder of Diane Kahler," Ophelia said.

Sandy's smile never faltered, and her eyes glittered with the news. "Is that so?"

"Yes. Beginning with what you were doing at the office of Barnard Financial despite recently being fired?"

"Why, collecting personal items from my desk." Sandy patted the open space beside her, and the poodle trotted across the room and hopped up to the couch. "As I told that very kind officer—Jones, I believe—I had such a sweet picture of Bijou at the conservatory that I couldn't stand to let Mr. Barnard throw away."

"And you didn't speak with Diane?"

"Well, I couldn't, you see. By the time I found her, she was already dead."

Ophelia frowned and sipped her tea. *That confirms who discovered the body.* "You don't seem very upset by this fact, Ms. Livingston."

"Oh, call me Sandy, please!" Sandy giggled and waved a hand of dismissal. "Of course I was upset at the time! But Diane and I weren't exactly close."

Ophelia replaced the cup on its saucer. "I've heard as much. I was informed that the two of you had a go of it on Wednesday evening."

The corners of Sandy's mouth twitched. "Ah. Did Larry tell you that?"

Ophelia seemed to have finally hit a sore spot. She pressed on. "What was the fight about?"

Sandy's bright smile dissolved into a thin line across her lips. The poodle whined and shifted positions to lay her head on her master's lap. "I don't believe this is pertinent to your case, Ms. Windsor."

"I would appreciate it if you would allow me to make that call." Ophelia locked her gaze. "Please, anything at all may help this case."

"If you must." Stroking the dog's fluffed fur, Sandy sighed. "Diane and I both worked for Barnard Financial for a very long time. I, however, held at least two years of tenure over her. On Wednesday, Diane received a promotion I'd been after for *years.*" Her tone soured. "A woman of such lascivious talents was a direct shoo-in, it seemed."

"*Lascivious?*" Ophelia frowned.

"My apologies. I know it's a difficult word. Shall I paint a picture for you?" The saccharine coating on her voice returned.

"That won't be necessary. However, do you have proof that Diane engaged in relations with your boss?"

Sandy cackled. "Oh, no. But *everyone* at the office knew it. Diane would flirt with any John, Dick, or Harry that gave her the time of day. My goodness, even Larry had his turn."

"Evidence, Ms. Livingston?" Sandy's demeanor set Ophelia's nerves on edge. First names felt far too familiar to share with an apparent rumormonger.

Sandy leaned forward and dropped her voice as if sharing a well-guarded secret. "Wednesday evening, after I was let go, I stayed in the parking lot for a long, long time. Just thinking about things, you know? What I would do after Barnard, whether they'd give me a good reference, how I would keep Kate on my staff—"

"And then what happened?" Ophelia interrupted.

Sandy pursed her lips but recovered quickly. "Well, then I saw Diane leave, and who was there to greet her? Half-sauced Larry, all prim and proper-like. Bowing when he saw her, holding an arm out for her to take. All chivalry and no security guard. Diane certainly did take that arm and led him to her car, and they left together." The sharp smile returned. "Where does a woman go with a tipsy gentleman, I wonder?"

Where indeed? "Can you please review this morning with me? From the time you woke up to the time you left the office?"

Sandy's sly smile returned. "I would love nothing more."

The tiny hairs on Ophelia's arms raised. Sandy may not have been an immortal, but she performed her perfect routine with terrifying effect.

"I woke up at six-thirty—two hours after I would set my alarm for work. This makeup doesn't apply itself, as I'm sure you know." Sandy blinked as if seeing Ophelia's face for the first time. "Or perhaps you don't. Anyway, I was so torn over missing my sweet Bijou's photo and my personal calendar that I settled for an easier look, skipped breakfast, and left the house at seven-fifteen. It seems you aren't fortunate enough to own your own vehicle, so allow me to assure you that it is exactly fifteen minutes to the office in a personal vehicle."

A few choice words and a tornado would engulf your house, Ms. Livingston. Ophelia took a deep breath and allowed Sandy's blatant jabs to tumble away with her exhale. "And between seven and seven thirty-five?"

Sandy furrowed her brow. "I walked to the office from my car." She clicked her shoes together, drawing attention to her three-inch heels. "Why run when you can strut?"

Uh-huh. "Can Kate confirm that you were here all morning?"

"Kate arrives at eight, but just ask Bijou!" Sandy scratched behind the poodle's ears. "We had a wonderful morning, didn't we, Bijou?"

Bijou made no move to collude Sandy's story.

It was a good alibi, but there were holes. And Larry hadn't told her the whole story. Diane Kahler's puzzle was slowly piecing together, but a few important pieces were still missing.

Ophelia clapped her notebook shut and stood. *Time to talk with Larry again.* "Thank you, Ms. Livingston. You've been a great help."

"I certainly hope so." Sandy kissed the top of the poodle's head.

"Please call the station if you think of anything else that may assist us in Mrs. Kahler's case."

"Of course, Ms. Windsor. Information is my specialty, after all."

Ophelia frowned and showed herself out.

"Mr. Hall, a word." Ophelia summoned Larry from his desk with a wave of her hand.

Larry's eyes widened, and he bobbed his head in agreement as he stood and stepped around to greet her. "Everything alright, Ms. Windsor?"

"Not quite." Ophelia frowned, noting the renewed thin sheen of sweat on Larry's forehead. "From what I understand, Benny's wasn't your only stop on Wednesday."

The security guard's face turned bright red, and the sweat on his brow intensified. "I-I don't understand what you mean—"

"Did you and Diane leave Barnard Financial together on Wednesday evening?"

Incomprehensible sputters and sounds of alarm dripped from Larry's lips. Ophelia waited for a solid answer. "M-ma'am, I'll tell you so long as this information doesn't reach my wife's ears."

Ophelia nodded. "All confidential, Mr. Hall."

He wiped his forehead with the back of his hand and took a deep breath. "Diane was a dear friend. After her fight with Sandy on Wednesday, I thought she could use a pick-me-up. And… Gosh, I'd be fibbing if I said I didn't hope it would lead to something more… I know that sounds downright awful of me, but I—"

"Mr. Hall. What happened after you were both in the car?"

"R-right." Larry shifted uncomfortably. "We did go to Benny's. That much is true. She looked dog-tired. Poor girl was working double shifts all week."

"Did she often work double shifts?"

"No, ma'am. I've never seen her here so much."

"Did she say what pushed her to pick them up?"

Larry nodded slowly. "She told me she was in a real bad place with her landlady—months behind on rent. I don't remember how many, I'm sorry," he said before Ophelia could prompt him. "I tried to cheer her up. Buy her a few drinks, you know? A-and maybe I was a little quick in my a-advances… Gosh, I was a downright drag when she needed me most. And then she… She left right quick after I suggested she could stay the night at my place."

Very smooth, Larry. "And that's the last time you saw her?"

"Yes. But… Gee whiz, there's one more thing I really think I should say." The flush returned, and he clenched his teeth. "You see, I went to play a few hands of cards afterward. Blow off some steam. And who should I see there but Jerry Kahler."

"Diane's husband?"

"The very same. Tossing chips on the table like he had nothing to lose." Larry ran a hand through his hair. "And it wasn't the first time I've seen him there, neither."

"What time was that?"

"About eight o'clock. Pretty late for me, but I just couldn't sleep. Not after that."

Gambling habit? Ophelia noted the time. "How long were you there?"

"I think I stayed until ten. Had to get back here bright and early, after all. Jerry was still there when I left."

"I see." *Wife's working double shifts while her husband gambles it away.* "You said it wasn't the first time you saw him there. How often do you gamble, Mr. Hall?"

"A few times a month, at most. Don't exactly have the salary to throw away more than that. I've got *awful* luck." He chuckled and shuffled his weight between his feet. "But Jerry was there almost every time. Makes a guy wonder."

"Interesting. Alright." Ophelia considered her notes. "Is there *anything* else I should know?"

"N-no. I think that really is all this time." Larry flinched and looked over one shoulder, then the other. "Gosh, are you being honest? None of this will reach my wife?"

"You have my word, Mr. Hall." *Though, these things almost always come out in the wash.* "Thank you again for your help."

"You're welcome. I'm sorry I didn't tell you the first time. Really."

"Call the station if anything else comes up." Ophelia turned and made her way back to Max's cab. A man who suspected a disloyal wife and had an unchecked gambling habit would have a lot of motive. Sandy was still a possibility, but it seemed like Larry was off the hook for this one.

"Playing errand boy today, hm?" Max grinned.

Ophelia slid across the seat. "Don't worry, Max. I'll keep the tips coming." She returned his smile and scribbled down the Kahler's address. "We're getting close. Here's the next address."

"Aye aye, Captain." Max tipped his hat. "Happy to oblige."

It was time to meet Jerry Kahler face to face.

Despite the close distance to Barnard Financial's offices, the Kahlers' neighborhood appeared a few updates behind the times compared to the upbeat suburban homes just down the road. Faded paint and roofs with absent shingles were commonplace on both sides of the street. Overgrown lawns choked automobiles that hadn't seen use for years up to their door handles, and rusted playground equipment littered every other yard.

As Max pulled up to the address, Ophelia spotted a woman with her hair tied up in rollers and wearing a wrinkled sundress hammering on the door with one fist while drilling a finger into the doorbell.

"Jerry! I know you're in there! You answer this door right now, or it'll be the heat knocking next!" she shouted. "Have you been wasting away your rent money again, Jerry? *Jerry*!"

"Looks like the landlady," Ophelia murmured.

Max chuckled beneath his breath. "Looks like bad news."

Ophelia fished a few dollars from her purse and passed them to Max. "Max, I need a favor, please." Ophelia gave him a series of quick instructions before leaving the cab. The taxi screamed away.

As the landlady continued her onslaught against the door, Ophelia whispered, "*Ecruli.*" She tapped three fingers to her left shoulder, then her right. A shimmering haze gathered around her on the breeze—it would shield her once from a bullet, a blow from a weapon, or a particularly brutal punch. It usually gave her enough time to react if anything happened. Usually.

"Jerry, my patience is worn thin. I'm counting to three, and I'm coming in there!" the landlady hollered.

"Pardon me." Ophelia paused at least an arm's length away. The last thing she wanted was for the landlady to shift her rage and destroy the barrier. She couldn't recast that spell for another hour.

"Look, I know I'm being loud, Margarette! But I need—" she began as she turned but stopped when Ophelia's face came into view. "Oh. You're not Margarette. Sorry."

Ophelia shook her head and flashed a wry smile. "I'm Ophelia Windsor. I would be the aforementioned 'heat.'"

"You're a cop?" The landlady raised an eyebrow. "Did someone call?"

"Not exactly. I'm a private investigator, but I'm working with Cicero Police. I was hoping I could ask you a few questions."

"Am I in trouble?" Her hands drooped to her sides, and the color drained from her face.

"No, Miss…?"

"Edith. Edith Green."

"Thank you, Ms. Green. Diane Kahler was murdered this morning," Ophelia replied.

Edith turned three shades paler, and one hand covered her mouth. "Oh, that son-of-a-gun," she whispered.

"Who?"

"Jerry." Edith pointed at the door. "He's been avoiding me all morning. I didn't realize that Diane… my goodness." She touched her forehead, chest, then both shoulders in the sign of the cross.

"When was the last time you saw Jerry and Diane?"

"Well, that's the thing. I live just there." Edith gestured to the house adjacent to the Kahlers' with a shaking hand. "They were fighting something terrible last night—I could hear it from my house. It was late, about eleven, I think." She clasped her hands to her chest. "This morning, their fighting woke me up again. I looked out the curtains, saw Jerry get into the car with Diane, and then they left. But I know he came home. I heard the tires squeal. When I looked again, he was letting someone else in." She signed the cross again. "I didn't think it was a police officer."

The officer that interviewed him. "Do you have a key to the house?"

"Y-yeah. 'Course. Right here."

"Would you mind letting me in?" Ophelia asked with increasing urgency. She extracted a pair of gloves from her coat and slipped them on. If it was as bad as Edith made it sound, she didn't have time for Jackson to get her a warrant. She'd need to find evidence immediately.

"Sure." Edith keyed the lock and stepped aside.

"Wait out here, please," Ophelia asked. "I don't know how it'll look inside."

"Don't have to tell me twice," Edith mumbled.

Ophelia crossed the threshold and was assaulted by the stale smell of old cigarettes and spilled liquor intermixed with dirty laundry and body odor. The living room furniture was covered in discarded shirts, jeans, and towels. Dishes covered every inch of the coffee table, stacked on top of yellowing newspapers.

"Hello?" Ophelia called, stepping over a pile of laundry. "Mr. Kahler?"

"Edith, I don't have your money!" Jerry growled as he rounded the corner from the kitchen to the living room. When he realized it wasn't the landlady, he froze. "Who are you? What are you doing in my house?"

"I'm Ophelia Windsor, Mr. Kahler. We spoke earlier."

Jerry ran a hand through dirty-blond hair. Bloodshot eyes sank deep inside dark circles. His fuzzy jaw suggested he hadn't shaved in over a week, and his crumpled clothes seemed well-worn. "I'll ask you one more time, *Ms. Windsor.* What are you doing in my house?"

Ophelia held her hands at her sides, palms forward to show she wasn't carrying a weapon. Well, not one he could see anyway. "It was brought to my attention that you and Diane had been fighting recently."

"Yeah? What couple doesn't?" Jerry narrowed his eyes. "That's why you're in my house without a warrant?"

Parked at the entrance to the kitchen was a suitcase with the top flipped open. Inside was packed with freshly-pressed clothing and toiletries. Ophelia tilted her head. "Going somewhere, Mr. Kahler?"

"N-no. Unpacking. Jeez, you writing a book?" Jerry scratched his throat.

Ophelia scanned the rest of the living room. Nothing was in its place, and every surface held a knick-knack or dish. "Edith informed me that you went out this morning. You told me you were asleep."

"I needed a breath of fresh air and a cup of coffee. Didn't know that was against the law."

Partially draped across the sofa was a large, crocheted blanket. Ophelia had seen many of its like. However, this one's end was stuffed beneath the bottom of the couch. As if shoved haphazardly into the crevice. Generally, it would have looked right at home in such a cluttered room. But the blanket masked small piles of laundry, and sheets of newspaper poked out from beneath it. This was a newer addition to the couch, and it was concealing something beneath it. "You went with Diane for coffee?"

Jerry coughed an incredulous laugh. "In case you haven't noticed, we only have one car." He followed her gaze. "Something I can help you with?"

Ophelia frowned and took a step toward the couch.

"I would appreciate it if you left my things alone," Jerry snapped. "I'll call the station right now if you don't leave. We'll see how you do in court."

"Just protocol, Mr. Kahler," she said. "I don't need a warrant with probable cause."

"There was already a cop here, lady. What do you want?" Jerry snapped.

Ophelia chanced another step and touched the blanket. "Just one more thing—"

Jerry bolted forward, diving to the floor and skidding through the piles of dirty clothing and trash. He tore the covering from Ophelia's hands and reached beneath the couch. When his hands came free, he was pointing a gun at her.

Ophelia stepped back, eyebrows raising. "Mr. Kahler, put the gun down."

"Look, lady, it was an accident," Jerry panted, eyes wild. "I can't go to prison. I didn't mean it."

"Let's talk about it—"

Jerry's hands shook, and he blinked furiously. "It all would have been fine if Diane just let me shoot Edith. No more fights. No more banging on our door." He shifted to his knees, maintaining his aim on Ophelia. "But Diane, she just... she just wouldn't *listen*!"

It was confession enough. Ophelia murmured, "*Raval noumath,*" and added a quick flick of her wrist. The gun snapped free from Jerry's fingers and soared into her own. He cried out, backing away from her on his hands and feet.

"Just what the heck are you?" Jerry cried.

"A private investigator," Ophelia replied easily, removing the clip from the gun.

"You don't know what happened! You weren't there! You have nothing on me!"

The front door slammed open, permitting an armed Lieutenant Jackson and another officer entry into the living room. Max's message had safely made it to Jackson's desk. That was a relief.

"I thought you didn't carry a gun," Jackson said as he assessed the situation.

"I don't." Ophelia spared one more look at Jerry. "It's his. The murder weapon. He confessed to the crime, and a witness heard it." She held up the gun in her gloved hand. Another officer grabbed an evidence bag from his belt and held it open for Ophelia to slide the gun inside. "Ballistics should be able to confirm that for you, and Ms. Green can give you a recount of what happened here."

"Thanks, Ophelia. We'll take it from here." Jackson nodded and approached a quivering Jerry. "You have the right to remain silent..."

Edith cowered in the corner of the doorstep, watching Lieutenant Jackson take Jerry into custody. She seemed too flustered to have noticed the gun changing hands. *Thank goodness.*

Jerry stared at Ophelia with wild eyes, his gaze constantly flickering between her hand and her face. "You're a *monster*," he hissed.

"I've been called worse," Ophelia replied. She waited until Jerry was nearly to the car when she turned to Edith. "Ms. Green, why don't we go to the station together?"

"O-of course. Right," Edith stammered. "My word, I never would have imagined..."

"Thank you for your help, Ms. Green. We couldn't have done it without you." There was nothing else to say. There was never a true justification for murder, and Ophelia knew that Edith would struggle with it for a long time. "Here. Follow me."

Max's cab was still parked on the sidewalk, and he grinned when they stepped inside the backseat.

"What a day, Ms. Windsor," Max said, sliding inside the cab. "Figured you'd need at least one more ride."

"You're a dream, Max," Ophelia replied, pulling a cigarette from her coat pocket. "Let me buy you a drink later."

"That'd be my pleasure, Ms. Windsor."

Edith rested her chin on her palm and stared out the window.

Ophelia took a long drag from her cigarette and sighed. She wasn't able to prevent Diane Kahler's death, but she'd found a quick resolution. She hoped Madeline would find some satisfaction in that when she called her later.

For now, Ophelia wanted a few stiff drinks and a cuddle from Figaro.

The End

THANK YOU FOR READING!

Thank you so much for reading the first short story of *Ophelia P.I.* We hope you enjoyed this paranormal cozy mystery. If you think others would enjoy this book, please take a few moments, and leave a review on Amazon, Goodreads, Barnes & Noble, or Bookbub. You can't imagine how helpful this would be! We read each and every review to help us improve on our writing, as well as give us more ideas.

MEETING RENEE: A PREQUEL VIGNETTE

Download for free at: amz.run/9DjL

In the heart of 1660s New York lies an enchanting secret hidden within Ophelia Windsor's apothecary.

Ophelia harbors a magical talent that transcends mere potion brewing. When a mysterious stranger with profound magical prowess steps into her shop, he sets up a meeting for her with the High Sorceress, Renee Swan.

Have you read the first book in the main series of Ophelia P.I.? If you haven't, check it out! It precedes the short story.

There are three types of series for Ophelia P.I.: main series, novelettes, and short stories. You currently read the first short story. Check out the others for more cozy mysteries.

MAIN   SHORT   NOVELETTE

Follow authors T. Lockhaven and Catherine LaCroix on Amazon, Goodreads and Bookbub to receive notifications of their new releases. You may also sign up for T. Lockhaven's VIP newsletter at:

twistedkeypublishing.com/tlockhaven

Be sure to check out T. Lockhaven's other cozy mystery series.

MERRY AND MOODY WITCH COZY MYSTERIES

- ⇛ Book 1: Potion Commotion
- ⇛ Book 2: Bittersweet Deceit

COFFEE HOUSE SLEUTHS

- ⇛ Book 1: A Garden to Die For
- ⇛ Book 2: A Mummy to Die For
- ⇛ Christmas Book 1: Sleighed

www.ingramcontent.com/pod-product-compliance
Lightning Source LLC
Chambersburg PA
CBHW050429110726
47899CB00008B/2907